MECHANICSBURG PUBLIC LIBRARY

30246000896863

E
ROB   Roberts, Karen J., author.
        The little blue dog has a
        birthday party

D1003182

8/2017

The Little

Blue Dog

Has a Birthday Party

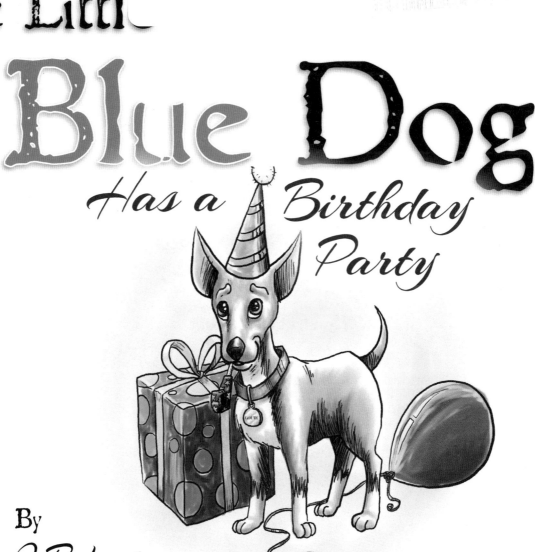

By

Karen J Roberts

Copyright © 2012 Karen J Roberts
All rights reserved.

ISBN: 061564712X
ISBN-13: 9780615647128

Library of Congress Control Number: 2012911781
TheLittleBlueDog, Wellington, Florida

Louie, the little blue dog, was a happy boy who loved to play, wag his tail and snuggle under cozy blankets. He loved his family and felt very safe with his two brothers, Mackie and Jackson, and his new sister, Roxie.

Roxie was a small, very sweet Chihuahua who ended up in a shelter, just like Louie. Louie remembered how lonely and sad he was living in the scary Shelter. He knew he was lucky to get a second chance the day he was adopted.

Louie's Mommy explained that there was a little dog, named Roxie, who needed a home. She was living in the shelter feeling scared and wondering how she ended up without a home.

He was overjoyed to learn that she would become part of his wonderful family. When she arrived at the house, all three boys happily greeted Roxie with welcoming smiles and wagging tails. They showered her with love so she would forget all about her time in the Shelter and look forward to her happy new beginning.

A few days later, Louie's Mommy picked him up lovingly, looked into his handsome eyes and said "Louie, your Birthday is on Saturday and we are going to have a party for you!"
This made Louie so happy! He gave his Mommy doggie kisses all over her face and wagged his tail in delight.

On the day of the party Louie woke up feeling extra playful because he knew it was his special day.

Oh, was he surprised when he saw the yard decorated with balloons, and a big "Happy Birthday Louie!" sign. But he was even happier to see all of his friends in the yard who were there to help him celebrate. He rushed out the door and on to the big grassy yard so he could join Mackie, Jackson and Roxie who were playing happily with all their doggie friends from the neighborhood.

Louie bounced with delight as he greeted his friends Sam and Otto, Chihuahua brothers who were from California, just like him. Pixie, Scruffy and Stanlee were there too, and Louie was so excited to see them at his party.

After lots of chasing and racing around the yard, and games of fetch and Frisbee, the dogs were all very hungry. Oh Boy, were they happy to see Louie's Mommy bring out a big cake for them all to enjoy together. "Happy Birthday Louie!" His Mommy said as the dogs barked and howled.

They politely gathered together for a taste of the delicious cake and a bowl of fresh, cool water. Louie was really enjoying the party, and he felt so lucky to be able to share his special day with his family and his favorite friends.

When Louie saw the big basket of birthday presents everyone had brought for him he couldn't help but think of all the sad and lonely dogs still at the Shelter. They all needed a home, and he knew they were in cages and not out playing and enjoying the day like he was.

Louie picked up a nicely wrapped birthday gift, and instead of opening it, he carried it over to the car and placed it on the ground.

Then he trotted back and picked up another gift and carried that one over to the car. Mackie, Jackson and Roxie followed Louie's lead and did the same. And before long, all the dogs at the party carried all the gifts and toys over to the car. They sat together and whined a little bit until Louie's Mommy understood.

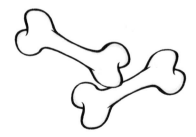

"Okay everyone, let's go to the Animal Shelter and donate all these wonderful presents to the dogs who are waiting for a home!" Said Louie's Mommy. She loaded the gifts into the car along with the left over cake, some dog cookies and treats, and the balloons and decorations. Louie and his party guests joyfully jumped into the car so they could take a field trip together to the Animal Shelter.

At the Shelter, Louie and his friends went around to all the sad and lonely dogs in the cages and brought them each a present. As their faces lit up with happiness, the Shelter dogs forgot their troubles for the afternoon.

They joined Louie, Mackie, Jackson, Roxie, Sam, Otto, Pixie, Scruffy and Stanlee outside on the playground. They ate cake, and played with their new toys and chased balloons. It was a wonderful afternoon for everyone, and Louie's heart swelled with joy. He had the happiest birthday a little dog could ever hope for.

When they got home, Louie's mommy hugged him tight and said "You are so kind and generous for donating all your birthday presents to the Animal Shelter. We love you Louie, and we are so blessed to have you as part of our family."

That night, exhausted from his party, and tucked into his cozy bed, Louie realized how lucky he was to have a home and a loving family. He hoped that more nice families would go to the shelter and adopt the new friends he made that day. They all deserved a second chance. He drifted off to sleep with a hopeful heart for homeless dogs everywhere.

The End

To learn more about Karen and Louie, please visit:
www.facebook.com/Authorkarenjroberts

49463660R00023

Made in the USA
Lexington, KY
06 February 2016